31 Days of Slavery

Code of Ethics

By

David Macon

Volume I

Acknowledgement

First off, all honor is due to the almighty God because, without him, none of this would be possible. I would like to thank my mother, my Queen, my true inspiration; you've been a blessing to my life. You will be forever appreciated, Mom. I also want to thank my father for the role he played in my life. I wish you were still alive to see the things I have accomplished. May you rest in paradise, Dad. I want to thank my brother and three sisters; you all also have been a source of blessings to my life and most of all, my two boys (David Jr and Davan) who are my joy. You all are my best motivators.

I would like to thank Janita Jones; a true dynamic black queen. You deserve the most credit for the completion of this project; truth be told, without your influence and extra push, none of this would have been possible. You had faith in me, believed in me, put up with my stubbornness, endured the struggle with me, and never considered giving up on me. You have contributed more than you can ever imagine in my life. You're a true best friend, lover, mentor, coach and guardian angel.

I cannot close without acknowledging Author Danielle Miller of DN Miller Publications & Services, who is also a black queen. You deserve credit for this project as well. You're a true sister-friend to me and my woman Janita, thanks for making this journal happen. You're definitely a true champion.

I do acknowledge that this journal might offend some high powered people, but that is not my intention at all. Nevertheless, keep in mind that this is what it is, and will continue to be, until I see a change.

David C. Macon

A word from my #1 Queen, my Mom (Geneva Macon)

My dedication to my son, who is the apple of many eye's and I'm so grateful to be his mom. A son who can move mountains with his words; now that's how powerful he is. I'm truly blessed and honored to have him in my life. Love you, Son!

Table of Contents

Introduction

I have learned to be fully accountable for my past actions. Throughout the course of my life, I have made many bad choices. These choices were the result of the many difficult circumstances we faced as a community and obstacles that were beyond my control, such as poverty within my community, limited resources, no motivation, and no guidance; except from my peers who were also like me. The insufficiency we experienced led me into practices such as ditching school and committing crimes. I was first arrested at age thirteen in 1988. I was released a few days later to my #1 queen, aka my mom. A month after my release, I was arrested again for another charge, grand theft auto. This is where it all started. But as I mentioned earlier, my lifestyle was the result of the many difficult circumstances we were experiencing, and the limited resources in our community. Where was the government? This journal is a self-help guide for every man facing trials and tribulations in our poor community. I exercise my first amendment to give my perspective of what 31 days of Slavery means to me. I welcome the reader to my world; *"Code of Ethics."* To learn more about **David C. Macon,** anticipate my project in 2021; it will give a deeper dive into my story. As this journal begins, read, write, take personal notes, and be real to yourself.

Negative aspects of prison: There are different kinds of negative people in prison: drug addicts, snakes, deceivers, thieves, people with mental illness, miserable people, dishonest people, unhappy people, the insecure and the arrogant. Lets not forget the people who are over-emotional, spies, the unpredictable, the uncontrollable, the envious and weak-minded followers.

Positive aspects of prison: There are different kinds of positive people in prison: Drug-free, loyal, open-minded, people that do good deeds, the wise, the knowledgeable, the intelligent, the independent, the honest, the generous, those that show gratitude, leaders, people with common sense, the trustworthy, the unique, and the strong-minded.

DAY 1 OF SLAVERY

Code of Ethics

(**Genesis Part I**): Let's begin this journal... are you ready for the truth? I made many bad choices throughout the course of my life because of the many difficult circumstances and obstacles I faced in my poor urban community, such as a lack of resources, programs, and positive guidance from the government. I recall being sentenced to juvenile camp as a teenager for six months; I ended up doing thirteen months because of my bad behavior. I was released from the camp in 1990. Four months after my release, I was arrested again, only this time, it was for a robbery incident. This time I was sent to California Youth Authority "C.Y.A." Later as an adult, I was convicted for a robbery and sent to state prison, and I was far from a model prisoner. I refused to abide by many of the prison rules. I always got into trouble, had my share of fights, participated in riots and many more. I was placed in solitary confinement numerous times. I have been released and arrested a few other times since my first adult arrest. And I just have to say, it is easy to get into trouble and damn near impossible to get out of trouble. To every action, there is a reaction. So you must stop and think before carrying out any action that will cost you your life or your freedom (put you in prison). I will tell you this; prison is the closest thing to Hell. In 2018, a beautiful woman came back into my life; she was my teenage love. Her name is Janita, and I call her my 'Guardian Angel.' We had many extensive conversations that have helped me in many ways. They afforded me the opportunity to step back, take a good look at my life, and, as I'd realized, the choices I'd been making had been totally wrong. I have now come to understand that I can do better than those choices. I have re-adjusted/ re-created myself into a newer and wiser man. I have learned self-control and let go of that aggressive behavior. I have obtained my G.E.D. and I'm currently enrolled in Coastline College.

The Song of the day while writing today's journal: "Best of Me
" -by Anthony Hamilton

_____

_____

_____

_____

_____

_____

_____

_____

_____

_____

_____

_____

_____

_____

_____

_____

_____

DAY 2 OF SLAVERY

Code of Ethics

(Genesis Part II): I am no longer accepting of the life of undeveloped potential I lived in the past. The old me has died and the new man I am has taken control. I have shifted my thoughts and my attitude towards personal growth, and I hold steadfast the values of my choices. I will continue to move forward with courage and faith. My future belongs to the new me. I can now look in the mirror and admire the person I see. Keep this in mind, I blame no one for the poor choices I made in the past. I was my own worst enemy, and I take full responsibility for my actions. Remember this, a man can change his life by changing his ways and the standards of his thinking. Never let anyone put the label of fear in your heart and make you believe you cannot become a changed man as a result. This journal is a self-help book, and it will bring forth knowledge to all men behind the prison walls and those in these streets of slavery powered by the racial profiling system. I exercise my first amendment of freedom of speech. This journal is my perspective and view of 31 days of slavery.

Spoken Words: "Never go back to what broke you, be strong enough to walk away and be patient enough to wait for what you deserve...its coming! Focus on your focus."

The Song of the day while writing today's journal: "Must be Nice
" -by Lyfe Jennings

_____

_____

_____

_____

_____

_____

_____

_____

_____

_____

_____

_____

_____

_____

_____

SUDOKU #1

		3				2		
6	9			2	8			3
2		1	7		3		5	6
4			5		9	8	1	
		6		8		4		
	1	2	4		7			9
3	7		6		5	1		8
5			8	1			7	4
		8				6		

DAY 3 OF SLAVERY

Code of Ethics

(After the Arrest Part I): First and foremost, if you do not have the cash to pay a lawyer to represent your case, which 90% of us from the urban community do not have most of the time, you are appointed a "public defender" who most of us call "public pretender," to represent you. 85% of the time, we do not get competent legal representation. These so-called lawyers go out for lunch with these District Attorneys (DAs), where they have extensive conversations about your case. They then meet up with you afterward and tell you about the offer the DA is willing to give you; it's straight-up bullshit! Then your public pretender will look you directly in your eyes with confidence and tell you how good the offer is, because of your extensive criminal background. Now keep in mind that this "pretender" of yours has not done any investigation on the case. So many underprivileged black and brown men, including myself, will meet with these public pretenders for the very first time, spend about forty-five minutes with them discussing the case and options before making a crucial decision that will most likely negatively impact us for the rest of our lives. Don't let the words "Public Defender" throw you off because, most of the time, the name "public defender" makes you assume they are defending you. You will assume you are doing the right thing by taking the pretender's advice. Keeping it real, unfortunately, seventy-five percent of these "pretenders" are incompetent. To be slightly fair, I have to say that one of the reasons might be due to the enormous amount of caseloads they have to handle.

Spoken Words: "Teach yourself the law and don't put your life in the hands of these public pretenders."

The Song of the day while writing today's journal: "Never needed no help" -by Lil Baby

_____

_____

_____

_____

_____

_____

_____

_____

_____

_____

_____

_____

_____

_____

_____

_____

David Macon

DAY 4 OF SLAVERY

Code of Ethics

(After the Arrest Part II): Let's continue from day 3. This is the reason why many of us will represent ourselves "Pro se." Pro se is a Latin word for *"in one's own behalf."* The right to appear **pro se** in a civil case in federal court is defined by statute 28 U.S.C. § 1654. We represent ourselves even though we really have no idea what the Hell we are doing; in my case, I knew it was possible in my heart. I had removed all doubts from my mind; I believed in myself 100%. In 2007, I was on trial for a robbery I didn't commit. I had a public pretender representing me at the time. I was found guilty. I was facing time, and I was meant to complete 85% of the sentence because of my criminal background. After the verdict, I asked the court to allow me to pro se so I could file for an 1181 motion for a new trial. This particular time I learned to conduct my own legal research. The judge permitted me to represent myself and I did that shit. Every day I was allowed two hours in the law library. I blocked everything out and dedicated all of my time, energy and strength into fighting my conviction. I was ultimately determined to give this crap right back to them. People don't see what we go through to represent ourselves. We have to get mentally prepared and learn a language we know nothing of, called "legal."

Spoken Words: "We must use our head for more than a hat rack."

The Song of the day while writing today's journal: "First Day Out" by: Tee Grizzley

DAY 5 OF SLAVERY

Code of Ethics

(After the Arrest Part III): Let's continue from day four; after two years of studying my case by learning all of the ins and outs about the law to support it; I then successfully filed my enormous "1181" petition for a new trial. I did this without the help from a lawyer or public pretender. From that point forward, I knew anything was possible. Once my conviction was overturned, the prosecutor offered me a thirteen years deal, and of course I turned it down. Two weeks later on my next court appearance, I was offered nine years, and again I turned that shit down as well. The following two weeks, I was offered six years with eighty percent due to my two strikes I already had. Since I was already in custody for three years, so the three years will be credited towards the six years, which will leave me with one year in half to do. Based on what I was up against ("racial discrimination & racial bias), I took the deal even though I knew I was innocent. But the odds were definitely against me due to past convictions having two other robberies on my record. At this time I had to use my head for more than a hat rack, and take that offer. I finally beat the wrongful conviction the prosecutor tried to throw at me. Put your mind to anything and believe in yourself.

Spoken Words: "Research, Review and Boss Up."

The Song of the day while writing today's journal: "We Be On It" by Def Loaf

_____

_____

_____

_____

_____

_____

_____

_____

_____

_____

_____

_____

_____

_____

_____

_____

_____

_____

_____

_____

_____

_____

_____

_____

_____

_____

_____

_____

_____

_____

_____

DAY 6 OF SLAVERY

Code of Ethics

(Mass Incarceration): Let's be real, the majority of the urban poor cities for the blacks and brown folks are considered the ghetto. Since the 70s, the African American community has been a target for the police, and crime had little to do with it. It was the color of our skin that regularly got us stopped and searched, interrogated, as well as abused. Then came the 80s when things only got worse. Law enforcement strategically organized a "get tough" act on African American citizens. Then came the 90s when there was an astonishing rise in prisons and jail populations with black and brown men. By the late 90s to this day, there is a stunning number of black and brown men in prison. As a matter of fact, we make up more than ¾ of the prison population. The Community Resources Against Street Hoodlums ("CRASH") was formed only in the ghetto in 1979. It advanced more in the 2000s and is dedicated to targeting the black and brown community. We must understand the role of this criminal justice system and look at it for what it really is, a "racialized system" to control the black and brown. It is a shameful and obvious legalized discrimination prison system. So far, we have been unable to dismantle the racial injustice system.

Spoken Words: "Wake up and realize we are all in the same struggle with this injustice system. Fight for your rights and don't settle for the bullshit"

The Song of the day while writing today's journal: "Superpower" by: Lil Durk

_____

_____

_____

_____

_____

_____

_____

_____

_____

_____

_____

_____

_____

_____

_____

_____

CODE OF ETHICS 1

There are 15 words hidden in the word search below, the words may be found across, down, diagonally and backwards and can overlap with each other. The hidden words are listed beneath the word search; circle the words in the word search as you find them and cross them out from the list.

```
R  E  I  D  L  O  S  R  O  T  N  C  E  S  R  Y
A  O  T  Y  N  S  L  L  R  E  C  T  L  F  N  D
B  E  O  T  O  T  C  R  I  M  I  N  A  L  O  E
A  U  C  I  C  H  I  N  H  I  I  E  R  T  I  O
O  R  N  R  N  G  N  E  N  A  S  E  I  E  T  H
L  I  U  G  T  I  A  L  G  T  P  C  E  A  A  S
S  N  S  E  D  R  P  O  G  U  N  D  L  A  N  O
I  G  G  T  E  D  E  R  T  I  O  C  A  U  I  L
I  R  N  N  T  V  N  A  I  C  I  G  I  Y  M  I
C  P  V  I  I  T  T  P  T  R  T  R  C  D  I  T
I  V  N  S  S  I  G  B  E  O  A  P  A  S  R  U
S  K  I  N  O  S  I  R  T  O  B  O  R  M  C  D
C  O  D  N  A  N  E  I  S  O  O  I  R  E  S  E
N  D  W  R  H  Y  N  L  S  D  R  I  O  E  I  I
E  L  G  G  U  R  T  S  B  O  P  D  S  I  D  A
I  W  T  R  U  S  T  W  O  R  T  H  Y  G  D  F
```

BLESSINGS	CODE	CRIMINAL
DISCRIMINATION	INTEGRITY	PAROLE
PROBATION	RACIAL	REPUTATION
RIGHTS	SOLDIER	SOLITUDE
STRUGGLE	TRUSTWORTHY	VISION

DAY 7 OF SLAVERY

Code of Ethics

(Plea Bargaining): Majority of us take deals for a crime we didn't do, and the reason for this is because a lot of us have an extensive criminal background/record. We have probably been convicted for a crime in the past that they are now trying to put on us now; like robbery, grand theft auto, attempted murder etc. Then you have these arresting officers who will find a witness to coerce and pay them to lie and testify against us if we choose to go to trial. So now the odds are definitely against us. Now the smartest thing for most of us to do when we are faced with this type of situation is to plead guilty and accept a plea bargain. Certain laws do not exist for 95% of us that have a criminal record; such as innocent until proven guilty, probable cause, guilty beyond a reasonable doubt. Let's be real, we are guilty the minute we are placed in cuffs. I can't tell you how many times I was stopped by a law enforcement officer just for walking down the streets with one of my homeboys, arrested for hanging out with a gang member while on parole. Bull Shit, Right! Even though I complied with all of his orders, I was still searched. I didn't have anything on me but cash. I was still sent back to prison for parole violation. (Racial Discrimination).

Spoken Words: "We must keep our head up at all times while going through this system!"

The Song of the day while writing today's journal: "Me Against the World" by: Tupac

_____

_____

_____

_____

_____

_____

_____

_____

_____

_____

_____

_____

_____

_____

_____

_____

_____

DAY 8 OF SLAVERY

Code of Ethics

(A walk in our shoes): I know many people might say; stop selling drugs, stop robbing and stop committing other crimes, and yes, you are absolutely right, those activities should be stopped. However, to those people who make such statements, do you know that: "being a black man automatically means you're (discriminated against)," "living in an "urban poor" community as a black man cause (racial bias). And last but not least, being a black man who has been imprisoned causes racial disparities towards you. So now that I have enlightened those who probably were blind to these facts I just shared, I would love for you to walk in my shoes for thirty-one days in my community, the "urban poor." Afterward, just maybe you'll understand our struggle. But until you can step out of that unambiguous world you live in, I refuse to hear anything those people have to say, unless you genuinely care and show concern. Also, you might just be willing to support the community's fight against discrimination & racism afterward. I also want them to keep in mind that if you have a felony on your record, it will be damn near impossible to get a good job that can support you and your kids. After prison, the next best thing for most of us is the illegal route we are used to, just so we are able to provide for our family. But with a renewed way of thinking and a new life, I can tell my people to strive for entrepreneurship; become their own boss.

Spoken Words: "Don't ever judge a book by its cover unless you read the entire contents."

The Song of the day while writing today's journal: "Lifetime" by: Maxwell

_____

_____

_____

_____

_____

_____

_____

_____

_____

_____

_____

_____

_____

_____

David Macon

_____

_____

_____

_____

_____

_____

_____

_____

_____

_____

_____

_____

_____

_____

_____

_____

_____

_____

_____

_____

DAY 9 OF SLAVERY

Code of Ethics

(Prison Survivor): The people you associate with are a critical aspect of prison life. You immediately recognize the good and the positive qualities in people. You must be intentional about who you surround yourself with. Avoid the miserable and unhealthy characters who are always unhappy. Doing time can either be hard or easy; it all depends on you and your character. You must use your head for more than a hat rack; "you must use common sense." If you want to have a smooth, easy time, surround yourself with the realness of "positive" people, but if you want to have a rough hard time, surround yourself with thieves and untrustworthy individuals that represent "negativity."

Spoken Words: "There will be many battles and struggles upon yourself, but you must never give up. Keep pushing and keep striving, and definitely keep your eyes on the prize."

The Song of the day while writing today's journal: "Open Letter" by: Lil Wayne

_____

_____

_____

_____

_____

_____

_____

_____

_____

_____

_____

_____

_____

_____

_____

_____

DAY 10 OF SLAVERY

Code of Ethics

(The courthouse): As for the courts, they are a part of this system of racial discrimination and racial bias. Instead of correcting the problem, they allow this shit to happen; just act as if they don't know what the Hell is going on in their courtroom. In a nutshell, the courts give these police and prosecutors the authorization as well as the discretion to racial profile those of us in the poor urban community, aka ghetto. They are all wearing masks – if only you can see their true identity behind these masks. God did not give judges the authority to intentionally put us in a system without giving us the right to prove our innocence. They need to go back to biblical history and read the books of "Judges" so they can understand that their purpose is to rescue the people from their enemies and establish a true justice system.

Spoken Words: "Let the Lord judge the criminals; Is it a crime, to fight, for what is mine?" Quotes by Tupac Shakur

The Song of the day while writing today's journal: "The Ghetto"
by: Too Short

_____

_____

_____

_____

_____

_____

_____

_____

_____

_____

_____

_____

_____

_____

_____

David Macon

DAY 11 OF SLAVERY

Code of Ethics

(Prison Survivor): Build a reputation as a good sincere soldier. Say what you mean and mean what you say. Be around people who are looking towards a new change in their life. We all make mistakes, however, don't live in your past. Surround yourself with people who are trying to better themselves; people who know how to think correctly. If you are really trying to better yourself, you must leave any negative circle you are in. Do a re-evaluation; re-check your mind, get it clear and get it right.

Analyze yourself and learn from your mistakes-here are some formulas:

#1: First of all, you must have a plan or idea in order to achieve a goal.

#2: Turn from bad habits into good ones.

#3: Be a visionary; have 20/20 vision.

#4: Be all about doing positive things differently and on a whole new level!

Spoken Words: "Be careful with being honest with people. Honesty offends some people."

The Song of the day while writing today's journal: "Who do you believe in" by: Scarface

_____

_____

_____

_____

_____

_____

_____

_____

_____

_____

_____

_____

_____

_____

_____

_____

_____

_____

_____

_____

_____

_____

_____

_____

_____

_____

_____

_____

_____

_____

_____

_____

_____

CODE OF ETHICS 2

There are 16 words hidden in the word search below, the words may be found across, down, diagonally and backwards and can overlap with each other. The hidden words are listed beneath the word search; circle the words in the word search as you find them and cross them out from the list.

```
T P E L E C C N O Y L T U R A P U S W
O L T F L L A I R T N E D M U U E R G
G O A E R E S E C E R V R B W U C V B
W P C N T W R P M S H A L O A P D C C
O N U E E B R E P R K I M R S L L T N
R L D S S I G T E S C D D U D D D N F
I T E S S D A O N P P O P O S X G P A
P M R O U N L O R D I P A A L N N T R
M A N J N Y I E N F O R C E M E N T E
L E C T V T T I K R T P I C N A P P K
R N L E A E N N T F P S U X I O O M N
I U I L N U A S V A O Y G I T G L B O
O R O D A P Y S E L F C O N T R O L W
P I E I S S U N E X P E C T E D T U L
V R A C T R I B U L A T I O N A N I E
S O H E U E R I E O P L R R W D B G D
N O M L T O V A S L A C X T P O H V G
C T A R H S H O N W R E Y R H G E T E
R N E L Z U J C L S V E V A F R T E T
```

CYA	EDUCATE	ENFORCEMENT
JUDGEMENT	KARMA	KNOWLEDGE
LAW	LOVE	PRISONER
PUBLICPRETENDER	SELFCONTROL	SUPPORTSYSTEM
TRIAL	TRIBULATION	UNEXPECTED
VIOLATIONS		

DAY 12 OF SLAVERY

Code of Ethics

(Prison Survivor): Always think before reacting; it will save you a lot of unnecessary problems. Sometimes you'll need to think for the next man as well. It is what it is. You must always carry yourself with dignity, integrity, and morals, no matter the circumstances, and most of all, keep your confidence up! Be good to people, and always treat others the way you want to be treated, because Karma is a Mutha Fucka. They say you reap what you sow; it doesn't take being a rocket scientist to figure out the basics of respect.

Spoken Words: "When you are in a position to help someone, help them. It shouldn't matter where they are from nor what race they are. And believe me, your blessing will come. Shit, look at me now - I know I shocked the world"

The Song of the day while writing today's journal: "Save Me"
by: Meek Mill

_____

_____

_____

_____

_____

_____

_____

_____

_____

_____

_____

_____

_____

_____

_____

_____

DAY 13 OF SLAVERY

Code of Ethics

(Prison Survivor): Start paying attention to you! Don't worry about what the next man got going on or doing. A lot of time, people miss their blessings or calling when it calls them, why? Because they are too busy worrying about the next person's business. Focus on you and fix what needs to be fixed within yourself. "Get to know who you are." Prison is a different world. Do not be judgmental or envious of the next man's bread; get your mind right and your priorities in order, make it happen for yourself and shine, shit. Rise up in this man cave. Learn how to stay concentrated on the things you got going on and stop being a hater.

Spoken Words: "You may not be able to control every situation and its outcome, but you can control your attitude and how you deal with it."

The Song of the day while writing today's journal: "Must be nice" by: Lyfe Jennings

_____

_____

_____

_____

_____

_____

_____

_____

_____

_____

_____

_____

_____

_____

_____

_____

_____

_____

_____

_____

_____

_____

_____

_____

_____

_____

_____

_____

_____

_____

_____

_____

_____

DAY 14 OF SLAVERY

Code of Ethics

(Prison Survivor): Be wary of friends, especially those you meet in prison. These guys are strangers, and you must view them as such; mysterious. This is because most of them have secrets and skeletons in their closets that might be very disturbing to others. Keep your guard up at all times. Prison is not a place to soften up. Do not put your trust in no one but you, in here. Don't get me wrong. There are some good ones in here, but it is rare; very few. Nowadays, things are so tricky; you don't know who is who (TRUST YOU ONLY). Never put too much trust in a so-called friend; envy is always present. Solitude is a must to get your shit back right; you must give yourself time. We all need some time to ourselves to think and re-evaluate.

Spoken Words: "Always expect the unexpected, "Shit happens!"

The Song of the day while writing today's journal: "Miss It" by: Yung Bleu

DAY 15 OF SLAVERY

Code of Ethics

(Prison Survivor): No need to feel sorry for yourself here. Pick your head up, and ask yourself, "Is this the life I want?" And I hope you look in the mirror and say Hell to the Nah. This is not the life you should want. I want you to say, "I am better than this." Now you must use your head, wisdom and intelligence to figure this shit out; how you can legally get the heck out of this hell hole for good. It should be your top goal and priority. Push until you accomplish your goal. Some people will be happy for your change, and some others will simply dislike the fact that you are transitioning into a positive person. But you must continue pushing right; do not let the negative people distract you from your destiny.

Spoken Words: "Don't come in and pick up habits that you didn't have before coming to prison."

The Song of the day while writing today's journal: "See you again" by: Wiz Khalifa & Charlie Puth

_____

_____

_____

_____

_____

_____

_____

_____

_____

_____

_____

_____

_____

_____

_____

David Macon

DAY 16 OF SLAVERY

Code of Ethics

(Prison Survivor): Prison is dangerous; it is a whole different world. It's like being in a jungle; everyone has to protect themselves. There are many distractions and diffusions. The only thing you have in prison is energy and time. You must use that energy wisely and that time productively. One way of doing this is by educating yourself, read a book, research, learn more about the law; anything is possible. Nothing can limit you when you feed your mind with knowledge. If you don't have a "G.E.D." or "DIPLOMA" or a particular trade or whatever you choose as your personal goal, you can achieve it in prison. I've done it, and so can you. This depends on where you are serving your time; just ask your counselor for more information. Don't get discouraged, I mean it! You must retrain your thoughts! In order to accomplish your goals in prison, your mind and concentration must be on one accord. The world expects the worst, but you must prove them wrong. They are definitely wrong. There are many smart and intelligent prisoners, don't be fooled by society or the bull crap statistics. You must use that energy wisely and that time productively. Keep yourself motivated while you're in prison. Have a queen close to you that will support your dreams and vision.

Spoken Words: "Great achievement is usually born of great sacrifice and is never the result of selfishness. A dream becomes a goal when actions are taken towards its achievement"

The Song of the day while writing today's journal: "Best of Me"
by: Anthony Hamilton

_____

_____

_____

_____

_____

_____

_____

_____

_____

_____

_____

_____

_____

_____

_____

_____

_____

_____

_____

CODE OF ETHICS 3

There are 15 words hidden in the word search below, the words may be found across, down, diagonally and backwards and can overlap with each other. The hidden words are listed beneath the word search; circle the words in the word search as you find them and cross them out from the list.

```
G K S I R F E M T J L A R T I U E
N T I G U I L T Y R U I S O I I M
I R R I E E O I E E Y S F E O A F
L A T E I T O N V S O M T R F T I
I N H D V U A I U E E L L I J P R
F S Y A O O T N I C B L I D C U S
O I O P R A L P I S R S E D Q E T
R T H N G A A U A M U U I U I E A
P I R E E O S M T R I N O T I P M
T O N S T E M S V I M R A R O R E
U N M S E F N I M A O N C L L U N
R S E E V T V C T E N N I S V I D
F R D N I E T E N N N T A Q I N M
I I T I R O S F E A I T A R C D E
U R B S C I I S O C T A O H Y N N
S N E U I K G K S A M O L P I D T
L I K B T I R S C C U A R E S K N
```

BUSINESS DIPLOMA DISCRIMINATE
FIRSTAMENDMENT FRISK GUILTY
HARASSMENT INMATES JUSTICE
NEGATIVE POLITICS PROFILING
REVOLUTIONARY SURVIVE TRANSITION

DAY 17 OF SLAVERY

Code of Ethics

(Decision Making Part I): Always try to say less than necessary because people will try to twist your words up and add to it when interpreting or explaining it to the next person; that's all wrong and shit. It's a dirty game. Keep your business to yourself. If you choose to share it with anyone, be prepared for a disappointment. These days, loyalty is very rare. Never let anyone figure out your movements; keep them off balance. Never rush to take anyone's side nor to commit to anyone (stay neutral and play fair in the sandbox). Always pay attention to your surroundings, and always be observant as well as alert. One thing you must understand is, your mind is a gift, and you must exercise it on a daily basis. Give it the proper nutrients, and also know when and when not to speak. Don't exhibit diarrhea of the mouth by being full of shit.

Spoken Words: "Don't expect to be respected if you ain't real with yourself."

The Song of the day while writing today's journal: "If I'm lying, I'm flying" by: Kodak Black

_____

_____

_____

_____

_____

_____

_____

_____

_____

_____

_____

_____

_____

_____

_____

_____

DAY 18 OF SLAVERY

Code of Ethics

(Decision Making Part II): There are many ideas to become successfully wealthy you can come up with (as they say), but let me break this shit down. All it takes to be wealthy is just that one idea that is backed up by some actions. You must think big. Do not deprive yourself of imagination. Your position in life depends on you. You and only you have control of your subconscious mind. There are no limits on thinking and understanding your big goals. It is through thinking and understanding that you will gain knowledge and wisdom. You must have a "goal" and the "plan" to take flight and achieve them. One must understand that struggles come with successes as well as failures. But through it all, you must not give up nor give in. Put in the same amount of work as you did when you were hustling. Put your idea to work. Every African American who is wealthy had to retrain their thoughts. Take those street hustle skills and flip it into a business mentality. See your hustle as a business concept. There are no limits on thinking and understanding if you conduct the proper knowledge (research). Mind over Matter! Create a vision. Put in hard work with self-discipline, and you will become successful with multiple accomplishments. It is a powerful equation. Write your personal thoughts in a journal. Evaluate yourself, then proceed to build a better and brighter future for yourself. And remember, any relationship takes partnership.

Spoken Words: "Shit, be happy even when there is nothing to be happy about. And most of all, keep your eyes on the Prize. Think Big and Think Positive!"

The Song of the day while writing today's journal: "Upgrade U" by: Beyonce ft. Jay Z

_____

_____

_____

_____

_____

_____

_____

_____

_____

_____

_____

_____

_____

_____

David Macon

DAY 19 OF SLAVERY

Code of Ethics

(**Prison Survivor**): Patience is a must. There will be many misfortunate and unhappy people amongst you. Truth be told, many of them have brought their misery upon themselves by their faulty and destructive actions towards others; it is called **"KARMA."** You must try to stay as far away as possible from this kind of miserable folks, real talk! Don't argue or try to help a person who fits into this category. It is damn contagious and dangerous, and you will suffer the consequences. Bad company corrupts a good character. It is called: guilty by association. Pick your association wisely. Never let a man get your words twisted up in some bullshit. Be real with yourself and to others.

Spoken Words: "No need for revenge, sit back and wait, those who hurt you eventually hurt themselves."

The Song of the day while writing today's journal: "All Falls Down" By: Kanye West

SUDOKU #2

8					4	2		5
				3				
	1		6		9		3	
1		4				7		
	6						4	
		3				5		6
	4		8		6		9	
				5				
6		2	4					8

DAY 20 OF SLAVERY

Code of Ethnic

(Prison Survivor): Prison is like a fucking roller coaster; it has its ups and downs. You must remain strong through it all. Stress kills. Let's not forget one thing, prison is not supposed to be a fun nor joyful ride. You are there as a punishment. Things aren't meant to be easy. This is so you won't want to return back to the hell hole unless you are caught up with the racial profiling bull crap-ass system. While doing time, you'll definitely need a support system, such as family, friends, and, most of all, a good strong woman to support you mentally; help you through the struggle you'll endure while serving your time. Most of the time, people fall or bend when they don't have a support system to help them through the ride. However, if such a person dedicates himself to growth, he'll become stronger mentally, emotionally, spiritually and physically.

Spoken Words: "People who hate you are always looking for other people that hate you. They are needing hater help. Stay strong doing your time."

The Song of the day while writing today's journal: "Turn on the lights" By: Future

---

_____

_____

_____

_____

_____

_____

_____

_____

_____

_____

_____

_____

_____

_____

_____

_____

David Macon

DAY 21 OF SLAVERY

Code of Ethics

(**AD-SEG "Administrative Segregation"**): Which means the hole. This is where they send you for disciplinary reasons; punishment in other words. This place will test your mental stability. It will either make you stronger or weaker. It can make or break you; it all depends on the individual. Personally, it was a building machine for me. And I say this because doing solitary time is definitely a reality check. You can use the time to really get to know yourself; understand who you really are without any distractions. I utilized those times to the best of my ability, (Mind-Body & Soul)... let's break this shit down;

Mind: I exercise my mind by doing a lot of reading, lots of thinking about ways to better and organize myself. I also make guidelines for myself and practice them while I have this solitude time. While in the hole, I realized how much I have achieved on a personality level. I now fully understand what life is all about. One thing is for sure, being incarcerated is not a fucking life. I made plenty of bad choices that got me where I am at now. And even though I had nothing to do with some of it, I have learned to fault no one but myself. We have control of our own mind and we must choose to use it wisely; the choice is yours. I can now say that I am truly ready to return back to society as a man with a plan, on top of plans, back-up plans, and never to return back to this hell hole.

Body: I exercise two hours straight every day in the hole or out of the hole, and I go hard. I use this as a self-discipline tool. As I am working out and pushing myself to the max, I say over and over again, "never give up nor give in, build to win with discipline." That shit is very therapeutic.

Soul: I am a firm believer in God; I pray every morning before I get out of my bed, and every night before I go to bed; prayers work. "Prayers go up and Blessings come down."

Spoken Words: "No weapon formed against me shall prosper."

The Song of the day while writing today's journal: "1942 Flows"
by: Meek Mill

CODE OF ETHICS 4

There are 15 words hidden in the word search below, the words may be found across, down, diagonally and backwards and can overlap with each other. The hidden words are listed beneath the word search; circle the words in the word search as you find them and cross them out from the list.

```
J T O E S S E S T R I V E U E
L N U R L F A I L U R E S S N
D V T R D B Y I N L H M T L N
P H I K E I F S F A W P T A D
A R U S G E F N R F O P C F W
S I E N I U N D O S P C E M I
A F N P T O W C S U O L N P S
S S E U A O N I E M E I A R E
S O R Z R R B A P N A S R A L
S E I K I L A L R R E E E A Y
E R I H E T I T T Y O R R M E
C I E Y E S A E I I I F G I J
C R A A H R R M C O R A O Y E
U I S T R O N G E R N S R B E
S A F N Y L L A T N E M U Y A
```

ACCOMPLISH   ENERGY   FAILURES
FUTURE   HARDWORK   LIFE
MENTALLY   POSSIBLE   PREPARATION
RETRAIN   STRIVE   STRONGER
SUCCESS   VISIONARY   WISELY

DAY 22 OF SLAVERY

Code of Ethics

(**Prison Survivor**): Calculate your own interest. Be observant about yourself, be kind to yourself and know your values. Accept responsibility for your own actions. Study both the positive & negative sides of you. Be real to yourself. Make a change within yourself before you go telling someone else what they are doing wrong. Take charge of your own life; this means having "self-control." It took me a long ass time to realize that the lack of self-control was the cause of one of my biggest downfalls in life. Trust you only, because people will disappoint you.

Spoken Words: "Everytime I watch the movie, "All Eyez on Me" takes me back to what Tupac mom said, "Your body is in prison, not your mind." Rest In Peace Tupac !!

The Song of the day while writing today's journal: "Dear Mama" by Tupac

_____

_____

_____

_____

_____

_____

_____

_____

_____

_____

_____

_____

_____

_____

_____

_____

_____

DAY 23 OF SLAVERY

Code of Ethics

(Release): The world you left no longer exists. Don't try to go back into society as the old you with your old way of thinking. Be flexible and open-minded so you can adjust to a new life and engage smoothly with the new world you meet. In the eyes of many, you are nothing more than a criminal. Society will be quick to label you a criminal and maintain such a label. It is up to you to be determined. It is up to you not to go backward. Show society that we are just as capable and worthy of being treated as human beings. Create a plan on how to actualize your vision after you're released. And believe me, you will need a plan for sure once you are back into the real world. From experiences, I can tell you this: it will definitely be a challenge. But you can do it. "Mind over Matter" Have a Queen that will be on your side and give you that moral support! Real queens are hard to find.

You must be ready for the 3 P's, Plan, Preparation, and Process.

 Spoken Words: "Make sure you have a plan before entering into society."

The Song of the day while writing today's journal: "We Got Hood Love" by: Mary J. Blidge

_____

_____

_____

_____

_____

_____

_____

_____

_____

_____

_____

_____

_____

_____

_____

_____

DAY 24 OF SLAVERY

Code of Ethics

(Prison Survivor/Release): Do not be afraid to show your good heart. It is always wise to be polite to others. Being rude only makes unnecessary enemies. Also, understand this: that person you call a friend can become one of your worst enemies. There are many disloyal, envious ass people in prison. Keep your guard up at all times.

Spoken Words: "Recreate yourself into a better you. Enter into society with a new identity and get yo money."

The Song of the day while writing today's journal: "Fortunate"
by: Maxwell

_____

_____

_____

_____

_____

_____

_____

_____

_____

_____

_____

_____

_____

_____

_____

_____

DAY 25 OF SLAVERY

Code of Ethnic

(Encountering Injustice): We must fight this racial injustice system. We must no longer go through life as victims of injustice & inequality. We must first have the right mental attitude. We also have to understand that we are really dealing with ignorant people. While dealing with these racist folks in America, we have to be strategic and well organized with our approach. For sure, it will definitely be an uphill battle with many challenges such as the racial injustice system, mass incarceration, racial profiling, black unemployment, lack of education, and housing in the "urban poor community." Let's get one thing straight; most of our young black men and brown kids in the hood join gangs because of the lack of after school programs to keep them active. We have to keep in mind that these crimes our youths are assuming are petty are not really petty as they think, because the law is constantly changing and failing our black and brown community in the process. They are now facing more time than they are supposed to at their age for such crimes. The fucked up part is, their brain isn't fully developed. The justice system and the government is targeting our community and we must not sit back and continue to allow this bullshit to happen.

Spoken Words: "Recreate yourself into a better you. Enter into society with a new identity and get yo money"

The Song of the day while writing today's journal: "Money Dance" by: Rick Ross

_____

_____

_____

_____

_____

_____

_____

_____

_____

_____

_____

_____

_____

_____

_____

_____

_____

DAY 26 OF SLAVERY

Code of Ethnic

(Crimes committed by Police Officers, Part I): Now let's talk about the crimes that were committed by the police officers; crimes they always get away with. 1) Racial Profiling: Law enforcement is known to discriminate on the principle of race when making traffic stops; the same thing applies when they stop pedestrians. African Americans are victims of racial discrimination, which clearly violates our equal protection clause of the 14th amendment as well as our 4th amendment. 2) Planting of drugs, weapons, and filing false police reports. 3) The killing of unarmed black men and women. Here are two recent examples of an unjustified murder of a black man and woman by a police officer, but of course, there are over many more. First example: "George Floyd" allegedly went into a store to purchase some items with a counterfeit $20 bill, which is considered an infraction/misdemeanor. Apparently, the store clerk called the police and reported the incident. Within minutes, the officers showed up at the scene. The officers became very hostile and aggressive and as a result, this black man lost his life over the prejudiced behavior from the police officer. That was a blatant intentional murder. George Floyd cried out to the officers, *"I can't breathe"* numerous times before he called out for his momma then said the last words, "tell my kids I love them." It took protestors and people from all over the country to bring this incident to justice, and also for all nationality to unite in unity. Now let's reverse this shit;

if George Floyd was a white man, they would have given him a citation for some petty shit like this. So, it is self-explanatory, 31 days of slavery.

Spoken Words: "Recreate yourself into a better you. Enter into society with a new identity and get yo money"

The Song of the day while writing today's journal: "Get up, Stand up" by: Bob Marley

_____

_____

_____

_____

_____

_____

_____

_____

_____

_____

_____

_____

_____

_____

_____

_____

_____

David Macon

CODE OF ETHICS 5

There are 15 words hidden in the word search below, the words may be found across, down, diagonally and backwards and can overlap with each other. The hidden words are listed beneath the word search; circle the words in the word search as you find them and cross them out from the list.

```
H Y D K E W S T I T E E S D O R N
C T H T U T N N I G R O E H O E B
E L A F L R H I L X C D E I S L S
S A T Y L I O T U I E R R C P A E
A Y E L O O I B E R A E C C R T K
C O R I D G D T M R S T S S O I I
R L S I E P Y R E P Y L E L B O R
I R I S R N L B O G L N E M A N T
F E E M Z R I N I P A W T E B S S
I E M H A E S S S R Y O L D L H E
C I O L A I C T R A O D E I E I E
E H D R B O N R P Y L K Y T C P R
A S E L W D E E T E S C E A A A H
Y E E A I I Y N A R I O A T U H T
T R R L S S H G O S D L S E S N Y
W D F H T E X T N R C W A S E R V
S U C R E L L H F P T A E T N I R
```

COWARDS — DISLOYAL — FREEDOM
HATERS — LOCKDOWN — LOYALTY
MEDITATE — PRAYERS — PROBABLECAUSE
RELATIONSHIP — RESPONSIBLE — SACRIFICE
SOCIETY — STRENGTH — THREESTRIKES

SUDOKU #3

9		6					4	
			3	1	9	5		
	5	8		4				1
	4	1				6	5	
2				6		8	3	
		4	9	2	8			
	6					1		9

DAY 27 OF SLAVERY

Code of Ethics

(Crimes committed by Police Officers, Part II): Breona Taylor"
who was also a victim of wrongful death in the hands of a police
officer. This successful young lady's life was cut short when the
Louisville Kentucky police officers deployed on a "no-knock"
warrant on her home. She and her boyfriend were in bed sleeping
when her front door was kicked in unannounced by the police
officers. Her boyfriend, obviously frightened, fired a shot out of fear
that someone had just invaded their home to rob and hurt them. He
did what any man would do to protect his queen and their castle. The
unannounced officer returned fire, shooting several times, which
fatally hit Breona. While she lay there after being struck by the
officer's bullet, she was still breathing for several minutes, however
not one of those asshole officers attended to her. Several minutes
later, she stopped breathing and passed away. The sad part about all
this is, these assholes raided the wrong house. Both of them (Breona
& her boyfriend) were completely innocent of any crime. Again, it
took a ton of pressure from the community and celebrities to get the
government to act on this unlawful murder. Just imagine how many
incidents like this have happened in the last thirty days across the
country; straight bullshit. These assholes were only fired from law
enforcement after taking a person's life. As of today, they still have
not charged these officers for the murder of (Breona Taylor). It was
clearly an unjustified murder of a young, innocent black queen. It is

definitely time for a change. It seems as if the government and political figures we have in power don't respect anything but violence. I honestly feel this is the time for a revolutionary movement. It is time for us as a whole to set aside our differences, rise together and demand that our dignity and our human rights be acknowledged, not for the blacks, but for all nationality.

Spoken Words: "NO JUSTICE- NO PEACE!"

The Song of the day while writing today's journal: "One" by: Busta Rhymes feat. Erikah Badu

_____

_____

_____

_____

_____

_____

_____

_____

_____

_____

_____

_____

_____

David Macon

DAY 28 OF SLAVERY

Code of Ethics

(**Behind these Prison Walls**): Is a smokescreen for a modern-day (slavery-system) of control. These racially controlled institutions were built for people of color and underprivileged lower class. Behind these secret prison walls is the journey to a new racial control system. Prisoners are forced to work, and when I say work, shit, I mean extremely hard labor. For example, a porter job is to thoroughly sweep, mop, clean and scrub the showers, wipe the outside of all cell doors, pass out the food, collect the food trays and trash. This shit goes on for about 5 ½ hours a day, and the pay is lousy, no more than $0.35 an hour. Chow hall workers are up at 4am up in the chow hall, preparing the food and trays for every inmate in the facility. All buildings have at least four hundred inmates/trays. Not to forget, each tray, pots, and pans must be cleaned after serving. Just to remind you, all of this hard labor is for a little pay. On January 1, 2020, it was announced that California's statewide minimum wage will increase at least $13-$15 per hour. The porters don't even make ⅓ of the minimum wage; do the math. Let's not forget that if you are assigned to any job, you must work, or you'll receive a disciplinary write-up; which means you will get more time added to your sentence and lose certain privileges.

Spoken Words: "Don't never stop striving, keep going"

The Song of the day while writing today's journal:
"Untouchable" by: Young Boy NBA

_____

_____

_____

_____

_____

_____

_____

_____

_____

_____

_____

_____

_____

_____

_____

_____

David Macon

DAY 29 OF SLAVERY

Code of Ethics

(Racial Profiling): Prisons are clearly a racial profiling controlled environment as well, filled with people of all color from the inner city areas throughout the United States. One will say the criminal justice system is supposed to control the crimes; I will say, step outside of that little box and look at the bigger picture to see it for what it really is. A comprehensive racial control system. Know this, the bigot prison officers who are there to police the convicts are no different from the law enforcement officers on the streets. They routinely harass and randomly search inmates. When out on the recreational yard working out and walking laps around the tracks, inmates are regularly stopped, frisked and searched by the correctional officers who are not even assigned on the yard to police. Ninety-five percent of the frisk and searches are ridiculous and random cell searches. Some of these officers are known for planting drugs, cell phones, making shift metal knives and falsifying incident reports. You will have inmates going back and forth trying to get rid of that charge, and ninety percent of the time, they lose in court. There is no win-win solution; it's all losses. This definitely makes it worse for inmates who have plans to get released. This can definitely add additional time to their sentence, from five to ten years—all controlled by a shark tank system.

Spoken Words: "Look at this shit for what it really is- step outside of that box and understand this shark tank system in prison."

100

The Song of the day while writing today's journal: "ApeShit" by: The Carters

_____

_____

_____

_____

_____

_____

_____

_____

_____

_____

_____

_____

_____

_____

_____

_____

_____

DAY 30 OF SLAVERY

Code of Ethics

(**Freedom Part I:**) Freedom starts with you and the way you feel. Don't let people nor society label your freedom. Freedom is a part of living, a part of breathing, although they want us to feel miserable and discouraged in this hell hole; don't let that shit get to you. Despite of what, keep your head up and understand that we are as important as they are, and have rights to freedom. Start off with educating yourself and focus on your case. Make sure you don't let the bull shit get to you. Even when it looks like the odd is against you, it's not! Stay determined and fight, don't give up on life! Make the best out of it, find someone that will have your back who is authentic and real, a real queen. Have someone on your side that is going to motivate you; that's going to make your time easy for you, less headaches. Life doesn't end here- keep that shit going! Rise to the top, stay true to yourself!

Spoken Words: "Your life is not over with- rise to the top whatever the circumstances are!"

The Song of the day while writing today's journal: "Song Cry"
by: Jay Z

_____

_____

_____

_____

_____

_____

_____

_____

_____

_____

_____

_____

_____

_____

_____

_____

_____

DAY 31 OF SLAVERY

Code of Ethics

(Freedom Part II:) Never criticize yourself about the decisions that led you in prison. Remember you still have people and loved ones who dearly care for you, so keep your head up while doing your time or fighting your case. Don't hesitate to talk to your loved ones, be self-encouraging and motivated. Prison can either make you or break you and don't let this shit break you. For those who are in the world, stay there because prison is not a place for you. You'll definitely have to follow the rules and don't lose your freedom by being in this hell hole. Take today's day journal and express your thoughts, be free!

Spoken Words: "For every action there's a reaction."

The Song of the day while writing today's journal: "Somehow Someway" by: Jay Z feat. Beanie Sigel, Scarface & Jadakiss

_____

_____

_____

_____

_____

_____

_____

_____

_____

_____

_____

_____

_____

_____

David Macon

CODE OF ETHICS 6

There are 15 words hidden in the word search below, the words may be found across, down, diagonally and backwards and can overlap with each other. The hidden words are listed beneath the word search; circle the words in the word search as you find them and cross them out from the list.

```
M S R O R P L A A G I T T T I U
I A F D I I S D A O U Y R N E M
S O O B E N N D N T W T E E S I
U O N T I N A F R T E I C G I N
N B L V I O I A T R O N R I C D
D C M L F M R M R S I G E L H O
E U I P N O L I R E O I A L U V
R H E G R K C U G E E D T E D E
S G C W E O E U F H T W E T M R
T R S E I T C U S W T E H N O M
O E E I E M A E T T A S D I T A
O G R C H N N R S V S L D T I T
D Y E R I S T O T S K E N S O T
I N J U S T I C E S C N L U N E
L I R A L L A E P P A E H N C R
N S T A N O I S I C E D I A T T
```

APPEAL	DECISION	DETERMINED
DIGNITY	FOCUS	INJUSTICE
INTELLIGENT	MINDOVERMATTER	MISUNDERSTOOD
MOTION	PROCESS	RECREATE
RIGHTS	STRATEGIC	UNLAWFUL

SUDOKU #4

6		1		5				3
		3		7				
						6		
	8	5		3	9	7		6
4			7		6			8
7		6	5	2		4	3	
		7						
				6		2		
8				9		1		7

RESOURCES FOR THE MIND

BIBLICAL VERSES:

Sirach 50:27-29

Daniel 1:20-21

Proverbs 9:7-18

Exodus 23:1-9

1 John 5:19-29

Ephesians 2:8-10

Isaiah 54:17

Psalm 20:6-7

BOOKS TO READ:

Stamped by: **Ibram X. Kendi**

Chained in Silence by: **Talitha L. Leflouria**

Slavery by Another Name by: **Douglas A. Blackmon**

Final Freedom by: **Michael Vorenberg**

University of Success by: **Og Mandino**

While He Sleeps by: **Danielle Miller**

OUR POWERFUL QUOTES:

"Remove all doubts and limitations from your mind." **-David Macon**

"Don't let the world define your freedom." **-Janita Jones**

"Never lose sight from developing a better you." **-David Macon**

"Your past has the control over your future." **-Janita Jones**

"You'll get out of life what you put in" **-David Macon**

"Never give up on the vision nor plan" **-Janita Jones**

"You must believe in your dreams and fulfil them" **-David Macon**

SUDOKU #1 (answers)

7	4	3	9	5	6	2	8	1
6	9	5	1	2	8	7	4	3
2	8	1	7	4	3	9	5	6
4	3	7	5	6	9	8	1	2
9	5	6	2	8	1	4	3	7
8	1	2	4	3	7	5	6	9
3	7	4	6	9	5	1	2	8
5	6	9	8	1	2	3	7	4
1	2	8	3	7	4	6	9	5

SUDOKU #2 (answers)

8	3	9	7	1	4	2	6	5
7	2	6	5	3	8	4	1	9
4	1	5	6	2	9	8	3	7
1	5	4	9	6	2	7	8	3
2	6	7	3	8	5	9	4	1
9	8	3	1	4	7	5	2	6
5	4	1	8	7	6	3	9	2
3	9	8	2	5	1	6	7	4
6	7	2	4	9	3	1	5	8

SUDOKU #3 (answers)

9	1	6	2	7	5	3	4	8
4	8	2	3	1	9	5	7	6
5	7	3	6	8	4	9	1	2
6	5	8	7	4	3	2	9	1
3	4	1	8	9	2	6	5	7
2	9	7	5	6	1	8	3	4
7	2	9	1	5	6	4	8	3
1	3	4	9	2	8	7	6	5
8	6	5	4	3	7	1	2	9

SUDOKU #4 (answers)

6	7	1	8	5	2	9	4	3
9	4	3	6	7	1	8	5	2
5	2	8	9	4	3	6	7	1
2	8	5	4	3	9	7	1	6
4	3	9	7	1	6	5	2	8
7	1	6	5	2	8	4	3	9
1	6	7	2	8	5	3	9	4
3	9	4	1	6	7	2	8	5
8	5	2	3	9	4	1	6	7

31 Days of Slavery (code of ethics) is dedicated to all men who are facing time in prison or in the streets dealing with racial profiling. To my soldiers (my boys) keep your head up and stay strong through it all. Know your rights!!! One Love!!

David C. Macon

www.ingramcontent.com/pod-product-compliance
Lightning Source LLC
Chambersburg PA
CBHW032122020726
47494CB00007BA/2202